W9-BWC-123

Koala

Rod Theodorou

Heinemann Library
Chicago, Illinois

Published by Heinemann Library,
an imprint of Reed Educational & Professional Publishing,
100 N. LaSalle, Suite 1010
Chicago, IL 60602

Customer Service 888-454-2279

Visit our website at www.heinemannlibrary.com

Designed by Ron Kamen
Illustrations by Dewi Morris/Robert Sydenham
Originated by Ambassador Litho
Printed in Hong Kong/China

05 04 03 02 01
10 9 8 7 6 5 4 3 2 1

Library of Congress Cataloging-in-Publication Data
Theodorou, Rod.
Koala / Rod Theodorou.
p. cm. -- (Animals in danger)
Includes bibliographical references and index (p.).
ISBN 1-57572-271-2 (library)
1. Koala--Juvenile literature. 2. Endangered species--Juvenile literature. [1. Koala. 2. Endangered species.] I. Title.

QL737.M384 T44 2001
599.2'5--dc21 00-063261

Acknowledgments

The author and publishers are grateful to the following for permission to reproduce copyright material: Ardea, pp. 8, 12; Ardea/Jean-Paul Ferrero, pp. 17, 25; Ardea/Francois Gohier, p. 4; Ardea/Martin W. Grosnick, p. 4; Bat Conservation International/Merlin D. Tuttle, p. 4; BBC/John Cancalosi, pp. 6, 9, 19; BBC/Georgette Douwma, p. 13; BBC/Tim Edward, p. 18; BBC/Steven David Miller, p. 20; Bruce Coleman/David Austen, p. 27; Bruce Coleman/John Cancalosi, p. 16; Bruce Coleman/John Shaw, p. 21; Mary Evans Picture Library, p. 22; FLPA/Natural Science Photos, p. 7; FLPA/Terry Whittaker, p. 24; NHPA, p. 15; NHPA/Martin Harvey, p. 14; Oxford Scientific Films, pp. 5, 11; State Library of Queensland, Australia, p. 23; John Waterhouse, p. 26.

Cover photograph reproduced with permission of Still Pictures.

Every effort has been made to contact copyright holders of any material reproduced in this book. Any omissions will be rectified in subsequent printings if notice is given to the publisher.

Some words are shown in bold, **like this.** You can find out what they mean by looking in the glossary.

Contents

Animals in Danger

polar bear

gray bat

cheetah

All over the world, more than 25,000 animal **species** are in danger. Some are in danger because their homes are being destroyed. Many are in danger because people hunt them.

This book is about koalas and why they are **endangered.** Unless people **protect** them, koalas will become **extinct.** We will only be able to find out about them from books like this.

What Are Koalas?

Koalas are **mammals.** Many people think koalas are bears, but they are **marsupials.** This means they are related to kangaroos, but not to bears.

Koalas like to live alone. They spend their entire lives in trees. They are **nocturnal,** so they are more active at night.

What Do Koalas Look Like?

Koalas are about the size of a small dog. Their fur is gray-brown, with white spots on their chins and stomachs. They have round faces and ears and a flat nose.

Koalas have sharp pointed claws and rough pads on their paws to help them climb trees. Their arms are almost the same length as their legs. This also helps them climb.

Where Do Koalas Live?

Koalas live on the east coast of Australia. Most of them live in Queensland. The koala is a national **symbol** of Australia.

Koalas live in places where there are plenty of trees. Each koala marks its own tree with smells and scratches so that other koalas will not go near it.

What Do Koalas Eat?

Koalas are **herbivores.** They eat the oily leaves of **eucalyptus** trees. They have special teeth to help them eat the leaves. Koalas sometimes eat leaves from other trees, but they like eucalyptus best.

Eucalyptus leaves are not very **nutritious,** so koalas sleep for up to twenty hours a day to save **energy.** They eat at night, when it is cooler, to use up less energy and water.

Koala Babies

Koalas **mate** between September and March. The babies are born 32 to 35 days later. **Female** koalas usually have one baby every one or two years. The babies are called **joeys**.

When they are born, the joeys are small, pink, and hairless. They feel their way to their mother's **pouch.** Then they climb in to feed on her milk and grow.

Caring for the Joeys

When they are about six months old, the **joeys** start peeping out of the **pouch**. They climb onto their mother's back and stay there for the next six months.

Koalas leave their mother and find their own home when they are about one year old. If the mother does not have another baby, they will stay with her for longer.

Unusual Koala Facts

Koalas speak to each other with grunts and soft clicking, squeaking, and humming sounds. When koalas are very scared they make a loud cry like a baby screaming.

After it leaves its mother's **pouch,** a koala never drinks again! It will get all the water it needs from the leaves it eats. Koala means "no drink" in the **Aboriginal** language.

How Many Koalas Are There?

Australia is a huge country. At one time there were plenty of trees to feed hungry koalas. About 80 years ago there were millions of koalas living all over Australia.

Today the millions have disappeared. The Australian Koala Foundation believes that there are less than 65,000 koalas left.

Why Is the Koala in Danger?

About 100 years ago, many people moved to Australia from other parts of the world. They brought diseases with them. Koalas catch diseases easily, and many of them died.

Millions of koalas were shot for their furs. By the 1930s koalas were nearly **extinct.** Because of this, there are very few koalas left today.

Koalas need trees to live in and tree leaves to eat. Many trees have been cut down to make space for towns, roads, and farms. This leaves nothing for the koalas to eat.

More towns are being built near where koalas live, and they are often hit by cars as they try to cross busy roads. Cats and dogs sometimes kill koalas.

How Is the Koala Being Helped?

Conservation groups are working to **protect** the koalas and the trees they need to survive. Many koalas live in special **reserves.**

Sick or hurt koalas, or koalas that have lost their mothers, are looked after at special koala hospitals. When the koalas get better they are released back into the wild.

Koala Fact File

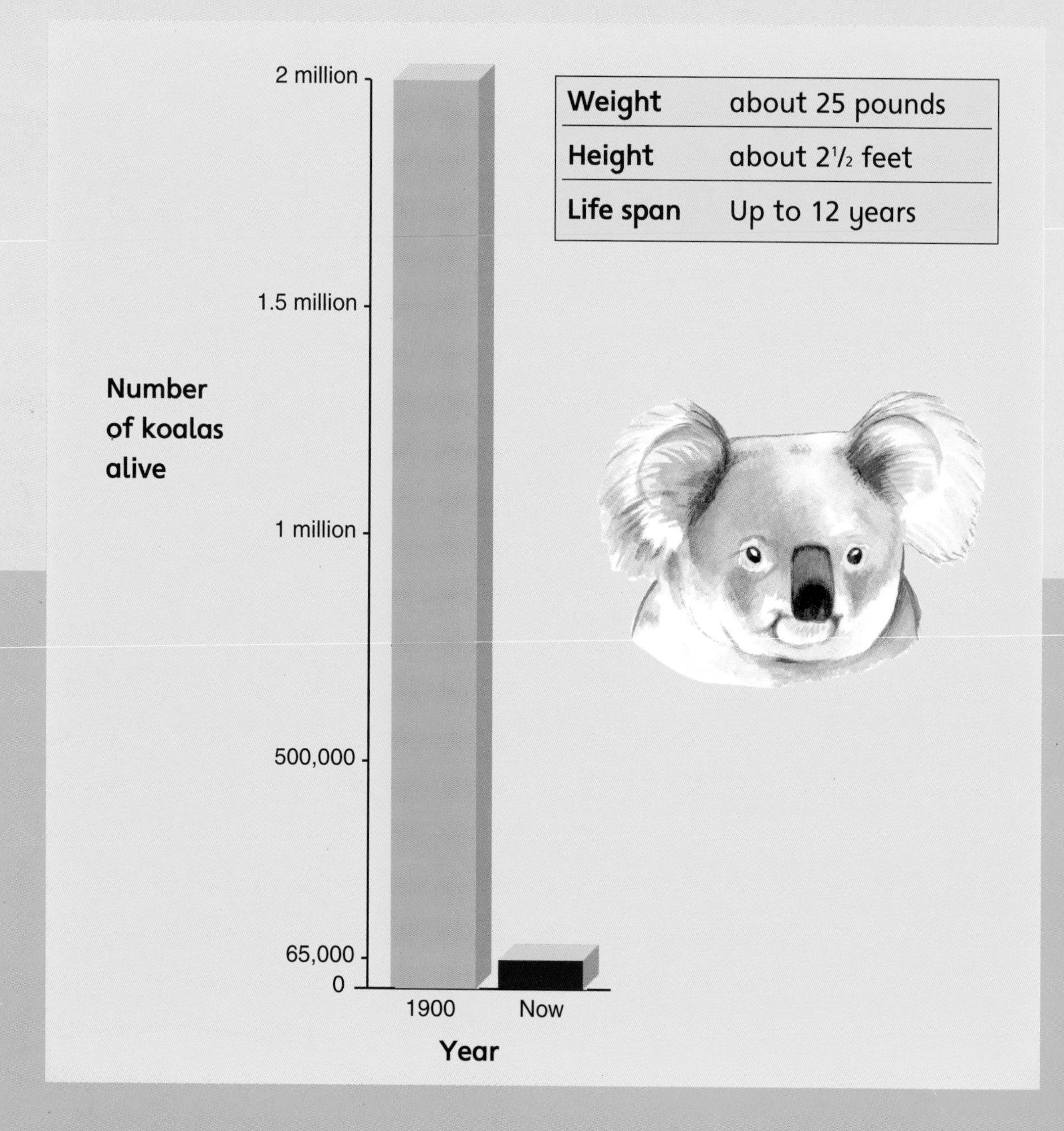

Weight	about 25 pounds
Height	about 2½ feet
Life span	Up to 12 years

World Danger Table

	Number when animal was listed as endangered	Number that may be alive today
Koala	40,000	65,000
Dingo	The dingo is not endangered.	about 350,000
Kangaroo	The kangaroo is not endangered.	15–35 million
Northern Hairy-Nosed Wombat	about 20	about 65
Platypus	The platypus is not endangered.	10,000–100,000

There are many other animals in Australia that are in danger of becoming **extinct**. This table shows some of these animals.

How Can You Help Save the Koala?

If you and your friends raise money for the koala, you can send it to these organizations. They take the money and use it to pay conservation workers and to buy food and tools to help save the koala.

Defenders of Wildlife
1101 Fourteenth St., N.W. #1400
Washington, DC 20005

Friends of the Australian Koala Foundation
c/o ATC International
2201 Distribution Circle
Silver Spring, MD 20910-1260

World Wildlife Fund
1250 Twenty-fourth St.
P.O. Box 97180
Washington, DC 20037

More Books to Read

Burt, Denise. *Koalas.* Minneapolis, Minn.: Lerner Publishing Group, Inc., 1999. An older reader can help you with this book.

George, Linda. *The Koalas of Australia.* Mankato, Minn.: Capstone Press, 1998.

Saunders-Smith, Gail. *Koalas.* Danbury, Conn.: Children's Press, 1998.

Glossary

Aboriginal	people who first lived in Australia
conservation	looking after things, especially if they are in danger
energy	power to move about and do things
eucalyptus	type of Australian tree with green leaves
extinct	group of animals that has died out and can never live again
female	girl or woman
joey	baby koala
mammal	animal with hair like a human or a dog, that drinks its mother's milk as a baby.
marsupial	kind of mammal that has a pouch
mate	when a male and a female come together to have babies
nutritious	food that is healthy and good for you
pouch	type of pocket on some animals' stomachs
protect	to keep safe
reserve	place where animals are looked after
snub	small and flat
species	group of animals or plants that are very similar

Index